O'Kelley Legends

MONOLOGUES

or

"How I Got Out of

Homework in

8th Grade"

by

Jordan O'Kelley

D1366405

DEDICATION

This book is dedicated not only to my parents, teachers, and educational therapists, but to all parents, teachers, and educational th'erapists everywhere who work with twice-exceptional (2e) students.

To all those families who work together to embrace their individual differences and celebrate their children's gifts and strengths.

This book is also dedicated to those loved ones who are now gone, whom I had the fortune to know and write about— Uncle Huggy Bear, Ms. Nellie, Carlo, and Aron Redner— all of whom were like grandparents to me.

To my educational therapist, Dr. Adrian S. Whitchelo-Scott, who first taught me that there are more ways to express myself through writing than with a pencil.

To my teacher and writing mentor at Bridges Academy, Stuart Matranga, who taught me that education might start in the classroom, but it doesn't end there.

To Dr. Jim Costello, Kim Prince, and Neuro-Fit Systems, who showed me that I could control and regulate my body, mind, and behavior through movement.

And, to the late Dr. James T. Webb, for his endless vision and inspiration in creating and sustaining SENG, Supporting the Emotional Needs of the Gifted.

"O'Kelley Legends Monologues" was first presented at Actor's Art Theater in Los Angeles on February 17, 2019 with the following cast:

Foreword	Tobin Hill
The Day I Managed to Scare the School	Norton Leufven
The Birthday Beans	Talia Basha
Irina's Gulag	Oliver Mather
Lost and Phoned	Rachel O'Kelley
Urgent, Don't Care	Joy Conrad-Mogin
A Birthday Surprise	Alex Wilson
Safe Baby Shark Bay	Julianna Riley
Patches	Emily Marsh
The Unlucky "Lucky Charms" Breakfast	Macey O'Kelley
Why Comedy?	Alexander Miller
My Run-In with the Police	Tobin Hill
Pranking Dad	Malia Bond-Blanc & JB Blanc
Fourth Grade Liars	Chris Richardson
The Kitty Story, Pts. 1 & 2	Julianna Riley
How I Spent My Summer Vacation	Brent Anthony

Directed by Jordan O'Kelley

CONTENTS

ACKNOWLEDGMENTS

How can I begin to say thank you to so many people who have made this book and play production possible. I am grateful to all of you, and I hope I can keep writing and producing, so that we can all work together again.

Thank you to my mom, dad, sisters, and to The O'Kelley Lab, for always believing in me, driving me everywhere, and for making my lunch. Thank you to all the real-life people who inspired me to write the original short stories from which these monologues are adapted. Thank you to my editor, Rosemary Nadolsky, and my assistant editor, Rachel O'Kelley, for your hours of proofing and notes.

Thank you to Jennifer Collins, Mark Tillman-Briggle, Michael Kallio, Dan Roebuck, Terry Hart, Mime as Therapy, Young Storytellers, Billy Riback, Davie Cabral, Duane Whittaker, Jolene Adams, Grady Lee Richmond, Bret Anthony, Gil Zuniga, Julian Zuniga, Lexi Shoaibi, Ramona Aguilar, Lindsay Kavet, Dr. Nicole Tetreault, and to all my mentors, our volunteers, actors, and their parents.

Please know that everything positive that comes from this book or from future performances of these monologues could not have been made possible without all of you.

INTRODUCTION

Hello Students, Parents, and Educators,

If you're reading this, it means you're holding a copy of "O'Kelley Legends Monologues," and perhaps you're thinking about performing them. I hope you do, and that you have as much fun as we did, watching these stories come to life.

I've adapted my book of short stories into monologues to help get the word out about what being twice exceptional, or 2e, is like. These monologues can be performed in a read-through format to support kids like me, who have trouble memorizing, or performed as individual monologues in drama class.

For our premiere read-through performance, we used a microphone and a music stand, so no one had to memorize their monologue. You can hear this performance as a podcast by searching for "O'Kelley Legends."

In going through the writing, audition, and rehearsal process with our cast of fourth through ninth graders, we found that it was the fourth and fifth graders who related to the material the most. We also found students who were interested in the project first, and then moved parts around in a more collaborative, non-competitive, repertory theater way, in order to cast the parts. Based on our experience, we think this show works best with elementary or middle school students.

Be creative! For your production, feel free to dress the stage as much or as little as you'd like. Have students wear what they are most comfortable wearing, or have everyone dress in a similar fashion. You can play recorded music between monologues, as the actors are switching out, and add lighting cues. You can cast a few actors to perform the whole show or use several students of different ages for each of the monologues, as we did. For "Pranking Dad," we had a parent read the part of "Dad," but we could have used a teacher or another student. The O'Kelley Legend monologues can be produced as a school play, community fundraiser, or both.

I hope you have as much fun as we did performing these stories and bonding with our cast and crew on and off stage. Please reach out to us at The O'Kelley Lab (www.theokelleylab.com) and let us know how your performance goes!

Break a leg!

— *Jordan O'Kelley, July 2019*

FOREWORD

What can I say about my first book? I'm lucky to have three important "M's" in my life-- my mom, Ms. Matz, and Maddie. My mother is one of the many people who inspired me to write this book— Why you are wasting your time listening to this, when you could be winning a round of Minecraft HG, I don't know. But, something I do know is this: Doing my homework now is a "get to" not a "have to." It was the greatest time I got to spend with my mom.

My teacher, Ms. Matz, is the one who let me escape the torture of handwritten homework and allowed me to write this book on a computer instead. And, Maddie and my fourth grade class are more of my inspiration. My favorite fourth grade memories are of listening to Ms. Matz read to our class.

How fourth grade could be such an amazing experience, I don't know. How making a deal to not do homework could turn into writing my first book, I have no idea. But it did.

To Ms. Matz, thank you for wanting me in your class, for putting up with all of my individual differences, for your wonderful personality, and for your skill as a teacher. I wish all gifted, twice exceptional, and special needs students could have a teacher like you for fourth grade.

To the smartest person I know, my classmate, Maddie— you have helped me grow as a person more than you will ever know, just by being my buddy and hanging in there. Where we go from here we will see… I hope fifth grade and the world continues to spin without an asteroid hitting it.

There are so many more "M's" in my life, like Maryanne, my school aide, and my little sister Macey. And my other little sister, "Machel." It's really Rachel, but I'm calling her Machel because of the "M" thing, and I don't want to leave her out. But what is the best is that, even though I can't tie a shoe, I have all of these people who love and support me enough to believe that I can write this book. Thank you all!

— *Jordan O'Kelley, April 2015*

O'KELLEY LEGENDS MONOLOGUES

THE DAY I MANAGED TO
SCARE THE SCHOOL

It was in 2010, some season that I don't remember, some day in that season that I don't remember. It was kindergarten, and I was climbing under the desks during carpet time. Apparently, classroom teachers don't like kids climbing under desks. So, sadly, my teacher said she was sending me to the principal's office, not for a penalty, but for a "walk and talk."

As a result, I lost my temper, and as the story goes, I wouldn't come out of the closet cubby where all the back packs and coats were stored. On my "walk and talk" with the principal, I was still really angry, so I said something I shouldn't have. I said, "You know, one day, I'll come back here, and I'm going to blow up this school!"

The principal's face turned white, and soon after that, my mom got a call.

The principal started the call by saying, "Excuse me, Mrs. O'Kelley, but, does your son Jordan have a chemistry set?"

"Excuse me?" my mom asked.

"Does Jordan like chemistry, or does he know how to make bombs by any chance, or does he own any?"

My mom's answer was, "Are you kidding? I'll be right there." But I really wish she would have said, "Oh yeah, I forgot to tell you about the Air Force jet fighter that my son owns and all the armed planes with five nukes each. That's why I open-enrolled him at your school. He was thrown out of his pre-school for making bombs."

Once my mom arrived at school, she said, "Really?" Then she asked, "What did you do to my son that would make him so upset that he would say something like that?!"

"Well, you see, Mrs. O'Kelley, he was climbing under desks, so we had to pull him out, and that's when he threatened to blow up the school."

"Why was he climbing under desks?!"

"We don't know…"

Later that year, my mom found out that I have loose joints, a medical condition that causes me pain when I sit cross-legged, like during carpet time. Geez, that would have been good to know before kindergarten. And to think it was all because of loose joints and watching too many "Road Runner" cartoons that, at age five, I managed to scare the school.

THE BIRTHDAY BEANS

It was my tenth birthday. I was super excited. After school ended, my mom picked me up and said she had a surprise for me, and it had to do with Harry Potter.

"Yaaaaayyyyy! I love Harry Potter!"

A few minutes later, we pulled up to a large building. Once inside, there was a red carpet looking thing— except it was orange and yellow. We walked down the hallway and went into the very last room on the right, and I saw HEAVEN. There were Harry Potter dolls, Hermione stickers, magic wands, and Norbert action figures! Squishy bed buddies. Hedwig cages. Postcard books. I loved it! But my favorite thing there were the Bertie Bott's Every Flavoured Beans.

So, we bought some Bertie Bott's Every Flavoured Beans and the game that comes with it! The game was called Bean Boozeled.

Here's how the rules work: There's a spinner and tons of beans. One person spins the spinner, and whatever it lands on determines what color bean you have to eat. Each color has two flavors. The flavors are:

Peach or Barf,

Licorice or Skunk Spray,

Juicy Pear or Booger,

Tutti-frutti or Stinky Socks,

Caramel Corn or Moldy Cheese,

Chocolate Pudding or Canned Dog Food,

Lime or Lawn Clippings,

Blueberry or Toothpaste,

Buttered Popcorn or Rotten Egg,

Coconut or Baby Wipes.

You don't know what flavor you get until you eat it. I got Lawn Clippings on my first try, and I actually

tasted grass. They actually worked! They weren't
fakes.

The game was really delicious! Well, mostly. At
one point, Rachel got Skunk Spray, followed by
Canned Dog Food. And while Macey was spitting out
the bad ones and only eating the good ones, Rachel
was following the rules and eating them ALL. Just
when the game was getting fun, Rachel said, "I think
I'm going to throw up." Not even joking, she walked
over to the trash can in the kitchen and threw up. She
waited another minute and then threw up again— this
time in the kitchen sink. By this time, my dad got
involved.

After Rachel threw up, I changed the rules of the
game to include eating marshmallows after any bad
bean, which came in handy when I got the Booger
Bean— well, until my mom took the bag of
marshmallows away.

But until then, you got to go to the marshmallow
bag and get some marshmallows. NOM NOM

NOOOOMMMMMM!!!!!   After all, it was my tenth Birthday!

IRINA'S GULAG

Once upon a time, about 10 years ago, there was a boy (me), who went to Irina's Daycare, which I now call Irina's Gulag. One day, while I was at the gulag, I climbed to the top of the Misty Mountains (the jungle gym outside). Looking out, that's when I realized, my house was only across the street.

Thinking my mom never left the house, I screamed "Mommy! Come get me!" for the rest of the time I was at the gulag, which was years. Every day at four o'clock, I would look over the hedge and scream "Mommy! Come get me!" If you're wondering why four o'clock, that's the time they let us kids go outside to play.

My mom said I was so smart for figuring out that we lived right across the street. I guess for being two, that's smart. She said that was my daily routine, and that if she was home, she could hear my little voice calling out "Mommy! Come get me!" That was my routine until the day I figured out how to open the gulag gate and let my little sister, Rachel, out.

That pretty much ended my days at the gulag, as my mom pulled up like a white knight in shining armor in her old white Toyota Corolla and saved me!*

*"The White Knight," *aka* "Betsy," is our old car.

LOST AND PHONED

When my mom wants to go to Souplantation for dinner on a weeknight, she's either tired or has had a really bad day. Sure enough, this particular night, she had just come from my second grade IEP meeting.

I've never seen an IEP meeting, but then again, I've never seen my mom want to make dinner after she's come from one. I can only imagine an IEP is a bunch of people I know at school, sitting around a table talking about me, as in, "Knights of the Round Table, unite!" I love talking about me, so that would probably be my ideal dream— and my mom's worst nightmare.

As we were sliding our cafeteria trays along at Souplantation, I could tell my mom was barely keeping it together as I took too many servings of beets. So, I tried to put some back. I packed on the mac and cheese, mixed two kinds of soup together (chicken noodle and clam chowder), and then the ice dispenser got stuck on the drinks bar, and my Diet Pepsi overflowed. The dessert bar was all out of chocolate muffins. Bummer. So, dinner was already kind of a disaster.

The restaurant was crowded and noisy, and all my mom wanted was some peace and quiet. Unfortunately, the three women sitting at the table next to us were having their own terrible day. Ironically, they had just come from a bad IEP meeting, too. They were very loud and upset, and they were talking very inappropriately about this poor kid and his mom.

Then we realized the ladies at the next table worked for our school district, LAUSD! As soon as my mom heard "Blah, blah, blah, LAUSD..." she tried to find another table, but the place was packed. Eventually, my mom couldn't take it anymore. She made us take our desserts to go, and she stormed out of the place.

Mom couldn't find her parking ticket to get out of the parking garage at the Beverly Connection, so she had to pay the max. She couldn't believe what had just happened and tried to call my dad as she was driving away.

What happened to my mom next I can only describe as an out of body experience, as she realized... she'd lost her phone. Let's just say, at this point, she was no longer keeping it together.

I calmly suggested that we go back into the restaurant to see if her phone was there. We did, and of course the people who had found it where those nice LAUSD ladies. It had fallen under our table. They had given it to the manager, who had put it in the lost and found.

That's why we call this the "Lost and Phoned" story.

URGENT, DON'T CARE

Why do they call it "Urgent Care," when it takes three and a half hours before they see you?

My mother recently took all three of us to Urgent Care, because she cares. But really, it was because my sister Rachel had hurt her foot at school. That meant no Minecraft for me after homework, because after sitting in the hallway outside the waiting room all night, there was no time for homework. My mom kept us in the hallway, because there were too many sick people and germs in the waiting area, and she was worried about my other sister, Macey, catching something. Macey is on medication to keep her immune system low, because she had a liver transplant when she was a baby.

Personally, I have no idea what my mom was thinking when she took us there. If you do the math, it would have taken less time if Mom had just waited until morning and had taken Rachel to the foot doctor then, while Macey and I were at school. It's not like Rachel was bleeding to death or was in any pain. You see, Rachel has this thing where she doesn't feel pain. So, what was so urgent?

Being a germaphobe, I was happy to be in the hallway, but I was bummed about there only being two chairs for the four of us to sit on. We had to take turns. To pass the time, we played every game we could think of, sang songs, and even made up silly dances. Afterwards, Rachel remembered there was a security guard at the front desk around the corner, five feet away, and surveillance cameras right above our heads. We then highly regretted what we had done, especially the silly dancing part.

We were feeling pretty silly right about the time they finally called Rachel's name. The exam room was crowded, and I don't think the doctor believed my mom when she told her that Rachel doesn't feel pain. The X-ray took forever, so we started asking Siri questions on my mom's new phone. I guess we were laughing too loud, because people were coming over to the X-ray area to see what was so funny. In case you don't know, you're not supposed to have fun in the not-so-urgent, Urgent Care.

All that waiting was a pain, but not for Rachel, even though it turned out that my mom was right—Rachel had broken her foot. After that, I wished I had given Rachel all my turns to sit on the chair in the hallway while we were waiting in the "Not So Urgent, Don't Care."

A BIRTHDAY SURPRISE

All summer long, just after third grade, I worked hard on creating the perfect digital birthday card for my mom. I had learned to code with Java earlier that spring. I was excited to use Java in my card, even though, in the end, I didn't end up using it.

It was close to mom's birthday, and she wanted to buy herself a birthday cake, so her party would go well. So, she went to Sweet Lady Jane's, and there she found it— the perfect cake.

It was a decadent chocolate Bundt cake with chocolate pudding filling and a light coat of powdered sugar on top. Mom left the cake on the kitchen counter. I looked into the box while Mom wasn't looking, and I was starving the second I looked at it. It was the most beautiful thing I'd ever seen. We all took baths, jumped in our pajamas, and dreamed of having a great birthday dinner with mom the next day.

As I was lying in bed falling asleep, I started to think about Mom's big digital birthday card surprise. Would she like it? Would she be proud of me? Was it worth me spending my whole summer creating such an epic art piece? Did I put too many fireworks in it? Was it too long? Would she get bored? Did she really like Minecraft, like she said she did? Or would she rather have flowers and candy?

I woke up and put the finishing touches on her card. I waited all day until her birthday dinner. After dinner, I showed her my epic gift. Her big birthday surprise! She said she loved it! But I think I got a little carried away with the fireworks.

Then she went to put candles in her birthday cake, and, unfortunately, she got an even bigger birthday surprise than my card. Someone… had come home late from work…and saw… the cake box… on the counter… and didn't realize it was a birthday cake…

and he cut a big hunk out of it! That someone was my dad!

I felt horrible for my mom, and even worse for myself, because it was a bigger birthday surprise than mine! But that was nothing compared to the surprise my mom gave my dad!

SAFE BABY SHARK BAY

When my twin sisters were about three and I was four, we asked our mom to take us to the beach. She agreed, but insisted we go to a beach that was baby safe and for young kids. After all, beach for us is the Pacific Ocean. My dad did a little research and came up with a good one. Oh– by the way, my mother is afraid of sharks.

The beach Dad found seemed like a baby pool, warm and shallow. We could wade safely, 'cause there were no waves to knock us down, and you could even see the bottom! Since the water was so safe, my dad decided to go back to the shore, sit down, and watch us from a little distance away. After a while, he might have even been drinking a beer, feeling so good about the fact that he had found such a safe beach for his family. It even had a little net across the swimming area.

Meanwhile, my dad blew up my cheetah print beach ball. So, we all got out of the water and started playing with it in the sand... until suddenly, the wind picked up and carried the ball into the water, where it quickly bounced away. I started screaming, "My ball, my ball! I want my beach ball!" My mom tried to convince me that it was okay if we lost it, because we had two other balls just like it at home. But I wanted THAT beach ball!

Finally, Mom said, "Okay, I'll try to get it." Dad stayed with the girls, while Mom and I quickly walked to the other side of the lagoon. Luckily, the ball began to blow back toward the shore. So, my mom went into the water. And, since it was pretty shallow, I followed her.

We hadn't gone too far into the water when we saw lots of little fish swimming really fast and so close to our feet that it tickled. I said, "Mom, look at all these cute little fishies! Wonder if I can catch them!"

She was still all about the beach ball, but I stopped to play with the fish. They were moving so fast that I couldn't catch them. It was almost like they were running away from something. Right about then, I looked up and I saw what they were running or swimming away from. So, I screamed out, "Sharks!"

There was a whole team of sharks swarming about five feet away from where my mom had walked out to. She had walked pretty far out into the water and was just about to pick up my beach ball. She quickly turned towards me and said, "Don't scream that out. It'll scare people. They're just little fishies." With a smile on her face, she proudly held up the beach ball and yelled out, "I got it!"

I said, "No, no, not the little fishies, Mom—the BIG fishies!" I pointed and could see her smile turn from confusion to fear. She instantly dropped my beach ball, which now went from bouncing across the water, to dancing on the dorsal fins of the swarming sharks. "My ball!" I screamed, "My ball!"

She screamed, "Forget it! Forget it! Get out of the water— now!" It was one of those mother-son moments that you never forget.

See, my mom is kind of grandma age, so she's not fast enough to play tag, but it turns out she can run fast in shark water.

She sprinted toward me and almost pulled my arm off as she yanked me out of the water. We got safely to the shore, only for her to realize her worst nightmare. My sisters were back in the water, splashing around, and my dad was drinking beer with his earbuds in his ears, awkwardly moving to some music. We started yelling, but we were too far away for him to hear.

As we passed people, we tried to warn them. We shouted, "There are sharks in the water! Don't go in!" But everyone seemed to know already. Turns out, the lagoon was a type of breeding ground for Lemon Sharks.

By the time we all got back to the safety of our blanket, I asked my dad to go back with me to see the sharks from the water's edge. There was even one guy filming them with an underwater camera on the end of a long pole. It was really cool to see them in nature, and not just on TV, or at the aquarium.

I never saw that beach ball again. But my mom had two more at home, just like she said. And every time mom starts to tell someone new the story of the "Safe Baby Shark Bay," they always seem to know exactly where the beach is, and that it's infested with Lemon Sharks.

PATCHES

My mom was big on buying multiples or getting more than one of something whenever they had a giveaway, like the cheetah beach ball from the Natural History Museum. I'm not sure if it was because she had three kids, or if it was something she had read in a parenting magazine, but she never had just one of anything. For instance, when I was a baby, my favorite bed buddy was a little brown and white stuffed dog, named Patches. I took Patches everywhere. I slept with him, I propped up my baby bottle with him, and I never lost him.

Which is where the story doesn't make sense, because everybody loses their favorite bed buddy at some point in their childhood, and their mom has to go to like ten stores or search the internet, until she can find another one.

I remember being very troubled about Patches one time when I was three, and I couldn't find him. Then I found him, but he didn't look right to me. His eyes looked a little different— too close together— and I told my mom that he looked sick, and we needed to take him to a doctor. Then, I had the thought that this bed buddy wasn't really Patches. I announced to my mother that this was not Patches, and I didn't want anything to do with this strange-eyed Patches. I was a very stubborn little boy, and not easily convinced.

Also, for the record, there were already three Patches at any given time, hanging out around the house. But I didn't make that connection until much later. I guess my mom had become an expert at keeping my Patches with me, my sisters' Patches with them, and not having any of the Patches in the same room at the same time. My mom is pretty amazing.

My mom eventually convinced me that, when my Patches was lost, he had been taking a bath in the washing machine, and that he had clearly had an accident with his eye while he was in there, and that's why his eye was not right and why he was so clean. Oh! Being three, I believed her.

There were a few other incidents like this over the years, but, overall, there was no reason to believe that there were more than one Patches. After a while, I did more and more things without Patches, and eventually he was living in a basket on top of my dresser. It wasn't until I was eight and reached into my underwear drawer and pulled out two brand new Patches with the tags still on them... What the heck!

My mom finally confessed. I had no clue that she had bought nine of them. No wonder we never lost them. Here's another clue that should have tipped me off— My twin sisters had the same bed buddy as I did, at the same time. Like we all picked Patches to be our bed buddy. My mom might be amazing... but that's just not right.

THE UNLUCKY "LUCKY CHARMS" BREAKFAST

Over the winter holiday break, the food war began in our house. My dad was determined to get our whole family eating healthier, while my mom wanted to make special holiday treats. The battle lines were drawn.

Mom wanted to make things like Rice Krispy treats, chocolate-dipped bananas, homemade ice-cream, and cookies. Yum! But when Dad heard about her plans, she got shut down.

Yet, Mom always has a Plan B. For instance, her secret stash of Lucky Charms cereal. Sometimes, when she went shopping at Target, a box of Lucky Charms would "magically appear" in our cart. And somehow, it would "magically disappear" when we got

37

home, 'cause Mom would "magically forget" to take it out of the trunk of her car. I'm sure it looked normal whenever we went out to the car with our cereal bowls...

On New Year's Day, lucky for us, Dad went for a morning run. See, besides eating stuff that tastes like it's been put through a de-flavorizer, my dad loves to exercise. He's got a rowing machine that I'm pretty sure is just a torture device. Oh, and he runs.

Sometimes after he's run his 3 miles, he looks more like he's just run a marathon— super sweaty and red-faced. I'm not sure how healthy running is for him.

My mom, on the other hand, hasn't worked out in twenty years, unless you count taking care of three kids as a workout—which she does.

As soon as Dad left, we grabbed Mom's secret stash of Lucky Charms from the trunk of her car and poured it into our bowls. Then my mom opened the fridge, only to find that the milk was frozen— unlucky for us. Mom always tells my dad not to put the milk in the very back of the fridge 'cause it'll freeze, but I guess he didn't remember this time.

Then Mom said something about Dad that I'm not putting in.

For a second, my sisters and I thought we were doomed. "How long does it take to defrost milk, Mom? When will Dad be back from his run? Can we put the milk in the microwave?"

Insert another "Plan B" by Mom. She took a knife to the top of the milk container, and cut through to some liquid, but not enough for three bowls. Then I asked, "What about a milkshake?"

She smiled and then did something nuts—delicious, but nuts. She dumped Lucky Charms into the blender and added the frozen milk. A short time later, we were sharing a Lucky Charms shake. It was "magically delicious," but not exactly healthy. My sisters said this would be a breakfast to remember, and they were right. Unlucky for us, Dad came home from his healthy run before we were finished with our unhealthy breakfast.

WHY COMEDY?

Why comedy? Why not drama, magic, dance, musical theatre, or singing? Why stand-up comedy?

Jim Gaffigan is the reason. Jim Gaffigan is the reason why I wanted to write comedy. He is super funny. And, if you're reading this, Jim, then all I've got to say is, "YOU ARE SUPER FUNNY! I LOVE YOU!" And if you're NOT reading this, then... super sad face.

Where do I get my ideas for my jokes? From me— how I look, my personality, my surroundings, and my relationships. These topics are what all successful comedians use.

So, for me, like Jim Gaffigan, it was a lot of fat jokes! I wasn't just too fat— I was too tall, and I was too nice. Here are some jokes from my first stand-up set. I hope you like them.

What's scary about being fat is I can feel my belly shake when I walk. Every time I take a step, I'm afraid everybody in a twenty-five foot radius is going to start screaming "EARTHQUAKE!!!" At my heaviest I was a 7.3.

What's weird about being obese is people always stare at my stomach— It looks like a balloon! One time a kid asked me if I could twist it into a poodle. So, if it popped, would air come out... or Wendy's cod burgers?

What's embarrassing about being tall is I look like I could cause some damage. I have to be really careful around fragile stuff, like ice sculptures or light bulbs... or the Great Pyramids of Giza.

I'm just too considerate. I'm always worried about hurting other people's feelings. Like when two different friends want me to sit with them at lunch. They're both like, "Sit with me, dude!"

I'm like, "I'll just stand, thanks." So, I do a lot of standing.

What's weird about me is I like to play video games after school to relax. Soothing stuff, like "Soothing Pond" or "Zen Garden"— or "Call of Duty: Black Ops 2."

It stinks that I can't build stuff in real life like I can in Minecraft. I can't just walk over to a crafting table and be like, "I've got two rocks and a stick... Let's build a house!"

I hate homework. It's so annoying. I'll do anything to get out of doing it. I even told my teacher that I'd write a book if I could get out of homework. So now I'm writing an epic... Delicious!

You know what's weird about the word "delicious"— and Jim Gaffigan knows this— is that somebody had to say it for the first time. Imagine some guy in 20,000 B.C. eating a woolly mammoth: "Oh, that was... delicious!"

I hope you enjoyed my comedy. Thank you, and goodbye!

MY RUN-IN WITH THE POLICE

My first run-in with the police was actually with a security guard at what used to be called Rexall on Beverly. Now it's a CVS. I was only four at the time and couldn't really make the distinction between the police and a security guard, so I thought it was the police.

I was shopping in Rexall— well, my mother was shopping. I was following her around, bored. So, when she reached into her purse to pay, I took off. By the time she looked down, I was long gone. She told security, they called a Code Adam, and the store went into lock down, kind of like our school drill. My mom said she was calling my name for quite a while, but I never heard her.

She eventually found me in the toy section. I was standing next to a giant box of light sabers. I couldn't understand why my mom was so angry at me. I tried to explain that I was bored, and I was looking for something to do to keep myself busy, and she should be happy that I was amusing myself. But she didn't see it that way.

She said that what I did was dangerous, and that she was sorry to say, but the Rexall policewoman was going to have to give me a ticket. "WHAT!?!?" The Rexall policewoman agreed, so she hauled me off to her office. I had to sit and give her all my personal information so she could write up my ticket. That seemed awkward— I'm pretty sure my "stranger danger" show said not to give away personal information to strangers.

My second run-in with the police was with a highway patrol woman, when we were on our way to Sacramento. My mom had gotten an appointment for my sister Macey and me to see a very famous neurologist in Sacramento. That's like a five-hour drive, one way. It took her six months to get the appointment, so my mom was all excited and very stressed out about getting there on time.

We were asleep when she first got pulled over, so we missed all the red blinking lights, sirens, and, I'm sure, my mom cursing. Mom got pulled over for speeding, but by the end of the conversation, she and the policewoman had discovered they had a lot in common. So, the policewoman gave us a police escort so we could get to our appointment on time. No speeding ticket!

Two weeks later, back in my kindergarten class, we were celebrating Community Week. So, a real policeman came to our class, and we got to sit in the police car and talk on the radio. When they asked if any of us had ever met a real police officer before, I raised my hand, since I'm not shy, and I said, "Oh, yes– and, I watched my mom talk her way out of a speeding ticket and get a police escort, with the red lights and the sirens on and everything!"

My teacher wrote my mom a nice note, telling her how entertaining my story was and asking her if it was true.

Quite a few parents over the next couple of weeks came up to my mom after school, asking her how exactly she talked her way out of that speeding ticket. Speeding tickets must be more popular than Code Adam tickets, because I've never met another kid who has ever gotten a Code Adam ticket. Yeah… right.

I recently got my mom to admit that there was no such thing. I knew it! But it worked. I never wandered away from her again.

PRANKING DAD

My family had to drive to Arizona for my cousin's Bat Mitzvah. Dad was meeting us there because he had to work the day we were leaving. On the way to Arizona, we got incredibly hungry. Like, desperately hungry. So, we stopped at the next restaurant we saw, which, sadly enough, was a super run-down Denny's.

As we ate, some weird people started coming in. Suddenly, Mom had to go to the bathroom. When she came back, she probably had the most amazing idea she ever had. "Hey, ya' know what would be funny? If we pranked Dad through texting!"

The following actual transcript of our text messages will illustrate what happened next:

Hi, Dad. This time it's Jordan. Mom is having EXPLOSIVE DIARIA in the bathroom. So, we could be a while :)

Is she okay?

There's an old man with a voice box thingy on his neck two tables down. I think he's got his volume turned up too high, the music in here sounds a little religious, and a bunch of motor cycle riders just came in, called Hardly Davidson club. The whole table of motorcycle riders are laughing a lot. They look like Uncle Jerry type guys. I'm sure Mom is fine.

OMG! The first time I ever saw one of those guys with the voice box thingy, I was on a train in Denmark, and it freaked me right out.

Just be nice to the bikers, and I'm sure they will be friendly.

There's a long line for the bathroom now. Should I send Rachel in to check on Mom? Rachel hurt her eye by the way. She grabbed the menu away from Macey and her eye looks bad. Do you think Mom will be mad? Rachel is worried.

Okay. Send Rachel in with the phone and ask Mom to call me. You and Macey behave. I don't need bikers texting their biker friends about the rowdy kids at the table next to them.

And, yes, Mom will be mad.

Mom's soup is getting cold, so I am eating it. She said I could, and Macey says it's okay.

I'm sure she won't want it If she's not feeling well.

OK, so now the janitor is at the bathroom door where Mom is. They say it's clogged. I wonder… : o

Oh boy. Is Mom okay?? Please tell her to call me when she can.

The soup was great though. I'm going to get it at the next Denny's. <3

Wow you are funny!

But can you drive a car?

I need you to take the phone to Mom and have her call me if she can. I need to know from her that everything is okay.

I'm dealing with Rachel, and her eye seems to be OK. I'm not going to tell Mom about that. She has enough to worry about right now.

The check came and they are waiting for our table. There's a line now for tables. I can't do the math, but I know where her money is. I found a $100 bill. Should I use that? That would be too much of a tip, right? My math sucks. Did you just try to call? How far away are you from where we are at Denny's? What time do you have to be at work? We miss you! Wish you were here!

So, after all THAT happened, we paid the price. And it had nothing to with the check.

We were afraid Dad might call the police and tell them to go to Denny's. He was already trying to figure out which Denny's we were at. So, we got back on the road, laughing about our prank, and when we tried to call him to tell him it was a prank, we had no cell reception. And that, ladies and gentlemen, was where it all went downhill.

We tried texting— didn't work. We had no way to contact him. We were surrounded by mountains in the desert. Now, we all actually started to panic. My sister Macey started crying, my mom started talking fast and loud, and I tried calling over and over and over. Rachel, as always, had no reaction whatsoever. Finally, we got through to Dad.

And that is why we vowed never to prank him again. I'm vowing again while typing this. I guess the prank was on us.

Bye!— *Click*

FOURTH GRADE LIARS

We've had a lot of family dinners. Each time, we talk about something different. My favorite dinner was the dinner where we talked about fourth grade liars.

In fourth grade, you hear a lot of things from your classmates— some of which, are lies. No, most of which are lies. Well, I don't want to point any fingers, so I won't say his name. I'll just call him, "Jeffadrome." Yeah, Jeffadrome.

One day, I was having lunch with Jeffadrome, and he said, "You know, when I was three, I rode a two-wheel motorcycle." At this point in the conversation, I already knew Jeffadrome was lying. Forced smile on face— I was doing good. That conversation ended pretty quickly.

Jeffadrome also said that he jumped off the roof of his house once. But just two days before, he said he didn't have a house. He really isn't a good liar.

He tries to lie about Minecraft. He once asked me, "Have you ever killed the Ender Dragon?"

"Yeah. Why?"

"What did you get from it?"

"A little portal with a dragon egg on top. Why?"

"I got a potion from it once."

"I can tell you're lying, dude. Potions are not valuable. And, plus, the Ender Dragon only drops the portal."

He also tried to lie about several other things, such as having Minecraft in the first place, getting mugged, and seeing a nuke. Mm-hmm. Yeah. Totally believe you.

It's really hard to be friends with a liar, because they're never trustworthy. You can't tell them to do anything without thinking, "Maybe I need to watch, and make sure they do it." There is something amazing about liars, though. They come up with all their lies on the spot. It takes a lot of creativity. You have to be good with improv. And I'm not. And you always have to be thinking.

I wish I had the ability to lie. I would tell Jeffadrome I went to a circus camp, where I rode a unicycle with an elephant riding on my back, while spinning plates. A circus and magic camp! While I was there, I learned how to make things disappear. I made my sister disappear for a week. I did all this without a Harry Potter wand.

I performed all summer, and I had enough money to buy a car. But I wasn't old enough to drive. So, I bought a snow cone machine. Now, my mother will deny this. So please don't ask her.

Hey— it's kind of fun lying. It's kind of like those Mad Lib games. Maybe that's how Jeffadrome does it. He's a professional liar.

I wonder, what's wrong with his life's true story? He's a creative genius, but the sad thing is, Jeffadrome has no friends. What happens to liars when they hit fifth grade? What happens to liars when they go off into the world? What's wrong with their truth?

THE KITTY STORY, PT.1

"Her name was Kitty. She came from a long line of kitties. Her mommy was a kitty, her daddy was a kitty, and if she had had kittens, they would have been kitties, too... but she didn't."

That's how "The Kitty Story" went. My mom would tell it every night when she put us to bed. After reading "Run Away Bunny" and "Goodnight Moon," she would tell "The Kitty Story"— the story of Kitty, our found cat.

One day, Mommy opened the door and saw this skinny, sick, dirty cat on our front porch— that was Kitty. My mom told Kitty and my dad, "I don't want a cat. I'm a dog person," but Kitty just kept meowing and wouldn't leave.

So, first my mom took Kitty door to door and asked all the neighbors on our block if anybody knew anything about this cat. Mom didn't even know most of those neighbors until that day. Then she took Kitty to our neighborhood vet and asked if they knew who Kitty's owner was. Unfortunately, Kitty didn't have a chip.

Then Mom took a photo of Kitty and had Dad make a poster that said, "Found Cat: Female, Gray Tabby, Needs a home." She put the posters up all over the neighborhood, but no one called. It turns out, when Dad made the poster, he got the phone number wrong. So, no one could call us.

"That was a mix up," is what my dad would say when he made a mistake.

Then Mom made another realization. Every time she opened the front door, the cat would run inside. It turns out that Dad had been secretly letting Kitty into the house. He had become attached, and Mom wasn't happy about it.

As my dad put it, "We were a house, but not a home, until Kitty came into our lives." Eventually, my mom agreed.

Kitty was our whole family's cat, but as the story goes, she would sleep under my crib and wake Mom up whenever I cried.

Kitty became my playmate. I would carry her around the house in my arms or pull her in my wagon. She was the greatest found cat ever. Together, we would watch our goldfish, Pearl, swim in her little tank for hours. Once Kitty and I sat watching my little butterfly habitat, as six butterflies hatched. Maybe I was watching them being born, and she was thinking something else, but we shared space every day for those first five years of my life. Kitty made our house a home.

THE KITTY STORY, PT.2

I was five when Kitty died. It was the saddest day of my life. I had known her my entire life, and I didn't know what it was going to be like without her. She had been sick for a while and had gone in and out of the vet's. Halloween was coming, and we were all about our costumes, when Mom took Kitty back to the vet's and was told that she should put Kitty down. We were going to see her one last time in the next morning and say goodbye, Mom said.

It was a Saturday morning before Halloween, and when we got to the vet's, they told us Kitty had died in her sleep. That was so like Kitty, making it easier on Mom. So, we took turns saying our goodbyes. I took a long time. She just looked like she was sleeping on that silver table, and they had wrapped her up so nice in a blanket and a towel.

I said, "I'll never forget you, Kitty. How could I, when my first word was to you. Remember? I said, 'Cat!' It's just so sad to say goodbye to you. I love you, Kitty, and you know I don't like change. But I promise, someday we will meet up in heaven. We will all be together again, just like yesterday, and just like in that home movie of us when I was two.

We will all meet up in heaven. Mom will be able to run after me, and we will get to play tag. Dad will have more hair. My sister, Macey, will have been born healthy. And Rachel, well, she's still Rachel, even in heaven. And you, Kitty, like the legend of the amazing found cat, will live on forever."

I made that promise to Kitty when I was five in that little room in that vet's office. I learned how to say goodbye to something you love by making a promise to let the goodness and the memory live on in my heart. I made that promise not even knowing what heaven or death really was.

It wasn't until much later that I realized that it's not the heart, but the brain that holds our memories. I hope Kitty will forgive me for not really understanding things I was talking about or promising. I think it's more common than you know that five-year-old's promise things they know nothing about. But you never hear people say at funerals, "I'll keep you in my brain forever— it's always in the heart."

Well, that's "The Kitty Story."

HOW I SPENT MY SUMMER VACATION

or
"Getting a Jump on Fifth
Grade Homework"

What better way to complete my fourth grade school year than with a summer vacation? — and an epic one, at that.

I could go through and tell you about all the boring details of the trip in chronological order...

But, summer break really started for me in Ms. Matz's class, during our end of the year potluck lunch. I was already on my second plate of food, which, when attending a magnet school in Los Angeles, could mean as many as ten different countries were represented on my plate.

As I looked over at my classmate, Maddie, I wasn't thinking, "Well, this is it, the end of fourth grade," but I should have been. I had sat next to Maddie all year, and in third grade, too. I was hoping to continue my great run of luck by getting sit next to her in fifth grade. She was my everything— peer model, classmate, reading partner, writing partner, therapist— as I was for her.

Just then, as I was looking at our plates, I was thinking about how Maddie and I were very different people. Mostly because I'm a boy on the spectrum (which sounds like a lab experiment), and she is a girl. My mom has always told me that I'm very observant, and at that moment, I was observing how different Maddie and I were.

Then, feeling like this time may never come again in our lives, I thought, I should say something— even though reading social cues has always been a challenge for me. I said, "Excuse me, Maddie... Do you mind if I ... Well, can I... Um... Well... Can I eat your last egg roll?" She answered, "Sure." I guess I had been observing how different our plates were for a while.

You can see why we were such a good team. And there we were, in the last hour of the last day of fourth grade. It's a magical and sweet time... fourth-grade. Even the bullies are just a little misunderstood, rather than rotten to the core.

Right around now, when everyone was counting down the minutes 'til school was over and summer break started, one person was holding the weight of the world on her shoulders— Ms. Bertuccelli, our Magnet Coordinator at Melrose Elementary. I bet she was downstairs in her office, sunglasses on, tissue box out, because she can't stop crying on the last day of school. She says it's something about the thought of never seeing the fifth graders walking through the halls again.

Luckily, Mom picked us up a little early and the 24-hour countdown for our epic summer vacation started. The trip was a big deal for our whole family, and especially for Macey. It was her first time ever going on a plane.

Well, that's it— the end of my fourth grade year, the end of my first family summer vacation, and the end of this chapter of my life. I'm looking forward to the next two months of playing on my computer and no homework. I'll do anything to get out of doing homework, even write another book. So, remember, if you hate doing handwritten homework as much I do, ask your teacher if she will let you write a book on a computer instead. She might just say yes, like Ms. Matz did.

THE END

ABOUT THE AUTHOR

Jordan O'Kelley was an elementary school student when he wrote his first book, from which these monologues are adapted. He recently completed eighth grade. Jordan lives in Los Angeles with his mom and dad, his twin sisters, and their new cat, Kitty Bean. Jordan is a twice exceptional (2e) student and still hates to do handwritten homework, due to dysgraphia. He is an advocate for 2e education and has written articles for 2e publications, which can be found at www.theokelleylab.com.

Made in the USA
Coppell, TX
05 February 2022

72954759R00051